Mommy, Why Am I Different?

Mommy, why am I different?

Copyright 2020 by Judy John-Styles

For information, please contact Styles Books Publishing.
Stylesbooksllc@gmail.com

ISBN: 978-1-7355915-3-7

This book is dedicated to my loving parents. My dad, Shamar Styles, for always telling me that I am beautiful. I will forever be a Daddy's Girl. My mom, Judy John-Styles, for always reminding me that I am fearfully and wonderfully made. My little brother, "Pop"- Shamar Styles Jr. who keeps me going.

I dedicate this book to my grandparents; Doreen Durand-Joseph and "Doodles"- Janet Thomas for your help and support to create a successful book.

My hair is dense and brown.
It curls when it's wet and super thick when it's dry.

Baby, your hair is thick, magnificent, and bouncy curls abound.

They say my skin is too dark and I make too much noise.

You have beautiful brown skin to match a beautiful voice.
We use lotion to keep our skin healthy and moist.

My eyes are too big and my lashes long and curled at the ends.

You have a special gift to see and discern who are your true friends.

I have thick lips with shiny braces and brown gums.

But you get to pick colorful bands that make your smile unique and fun.

I have long legs, with a size 8 shoe in the 6th grade.

Life would be boring if we were all the same, I love the way you are made.

I don't fit in at school, I always stand out.

Will you be a God pleaser or a people pleaser?
What will you choose to be about?

Mommy, why am I different?
I am different because I am fearfully and
wonderfully made.
I am royalty!
I try to follow the rules.
And I am not afraid.
I am super smart.
I have a big heart.
I am a Christian who loves God.
Changing who I am is
not worth it just
to have a squad!

Letter to the reader:

My name is Sarai Styles, I am 12 years old. I am a young black girl who wants to let all girls know that it is OK to be different. I want to let young girls know to always feel and be confident in themselves and understand that what you look like on the outside does not matter. As long as you keep your head up high and know that you are fearfully and wonderfully made.

Sometimes it is hard to feel or know you are beautiful because you may think that others are prettier than you or better than you, and that is not true because you're perfect just the way you are.

I am different because:

_____

_____

_____

_____

_____

_____

_____

_____

_____

_____

_____

_____

_____

_____

I feel brave:

_____

_____

_____

_____

_____

_____

_____

_____

_____

_____

_____

_____

I am confident when:

_____

_____

_____

_____

_____

_____

_____

_____

_____

_____

_____

_____

_____

_____

Acknowledgement

Destiny Salter, thank you for your expertise. You rock!

Stav Sachdev, we appreciate your support and taking this journey with us.

Grandma, we could not have done this without you! You are amazing!

Flash Animation and DHTML

ROCKPORT
PUBLISHERS

WEB SITE GRAPHICS

The Best Work from the Web
by RICHARD KARL DANIELSON

Macromedia is a registered trademark and Flash is
a trademark of Macromedia Inc.

First published in the United States of America by:
Rockport Publishers, Inc.
33 Commercial Street
Gloucester, Massachusetts 01930-5089
Telephone
(978) 282-9590
Facsimile
(978) 283-2742
www.rockpub.com

ISBN 1-56496-722-0

10 9 8 7 6 5 4 3 2 1

Designer: Daniel Donnelly
Layout: Cathy Kelley Graphic Design
Cover Image: Madison Design and Advertising

Printed in China.

" flash can manipulate that image mathematically, reducing bandwidth geometrically. seemingly overnight, the internet has started moving "

introduction

we are in the midst of the internet revolution.

The first major leap forward in that revolution is the advent of Macromedia's Flash. Vector graphics have changed, and will continue to change, the face of the Internet. Unshackled from frames and thumbnails, the Web is rapidly reaching its potential for design and interactivity.

The Internet of only a few years ago—even last year—was essentially a text-based medium. While there were visionary designers and photo-heavy Web sites, it wasn't until some programmers started fooling around with the early versions of Flash that progressive, interactive images started to appear. With vector graphics, once an image is loaded into your cache, Flash can manipulate that image mathematically, reducing bandwidth geometrically. Seemingly overnight, the Internet has started moving.

Flash is also a streaming medium that has enabled sound beyond the quality of .midi files. This ability has paved the way for DJs and music studios to go online and added an entertaining new element to every "shocked" site.

One of the greatest strengths of Flash is its versatility. Color palettes, fonts, and images can be imported from virtually anywhere. Flash animations can stand alone as in a Web page, or be confined to a window or frame. The options are almost as limitless as a designer's or an artist's imagination.

The sites in this book have been culled from the best of those new artists, programmers, and designers—the ones who aren't thinking in terms of what the Internet can do, but what it could and should do. These people are the Cézannes and Picassos of the Internet generation, because we truly are watching the birth of a new art form. Flash is the innovation that will reflect our times in the way that cubism or abstraction defined theirs.

THIS SITE SPEAKS *shockwave flash*
DOES YOUR BROWSER?

Title
Andy Lim
URL
andy.artdirectors.com/
Design Firm
Embedded Wireless Labs

Just about everyone has Shockwave Flash installed on their browsers today, but there are still a few uninitiated users out there. For those unlucky people sites have to have these "Check for shockwave" pages. At least, Andy Lim has created a screen that draws you into their overall design concept immediately.

Title
partyflights
URL
www.party-flights.com/
Design Firm
Amphion Multi Media

The cliché says that you only have one chance to make a first impression. Successful design should begin at the beginning, but sometimes it seems as though every site has the same "now loading" screen, as though those words were an Internet standard. Partyflights avoids this common pitfall by switching the familiar "now loading" to "now boarding," drawing the viewer immediately into the Partyflights concept. The simple jet illustration takes seconds to load and gives us something to look at while the rest of the site loads.

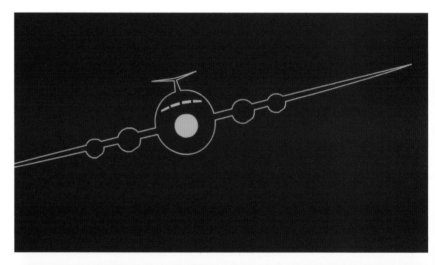

ALL PARTYFLIGHT PASSENGERS.

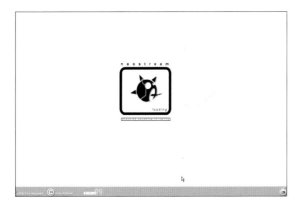

title
Neostream
URL
www.neostream.com/
Design firm
Neostream interactive

Neostream has the greatest loading screen to date. In the short time that this site takes to load, an animated head that gets "shocked" to life entertains the viewer. Using Flash, an animation of this type is about the same size as a standard animated .gif.

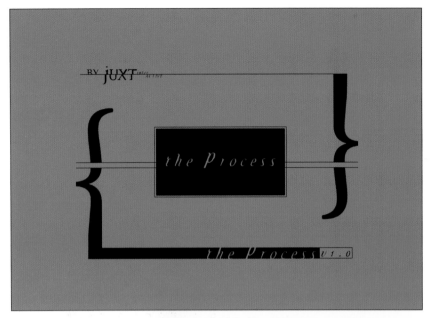

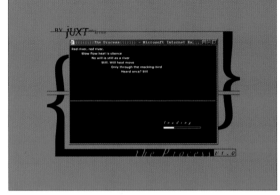

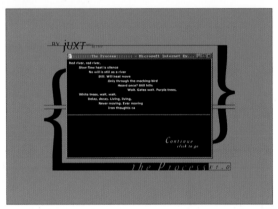

title
juxt interactive
URL
www.juxtinteractive.com/
Design firm
juxt interactive

Juxt Interactive is another well-designed Web site that eschews the over-used "Now loading" screen. Instead, this site gives the viewer a little poem. This screen is so effective that even after the Flash animation has loaded, users wait to read the whole poem.

title
The process
URL
www.juxtinteractive.com/
Design firm
juxt interactive

"All things are in process...The question is who controls the process?" A simple, repeating tag line tells the philosophy of the company in a memorable fashion. Created using Flash and JavaScript, The Process is an elegant site. Everything moves, but the focus remains on the iconic images. In addition, the colors used are rarely seen on the Internet.

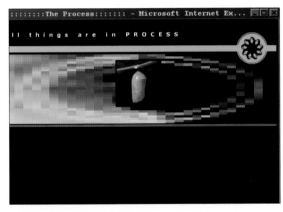

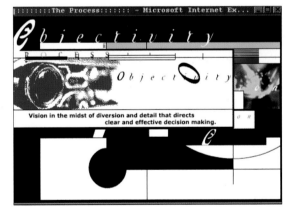

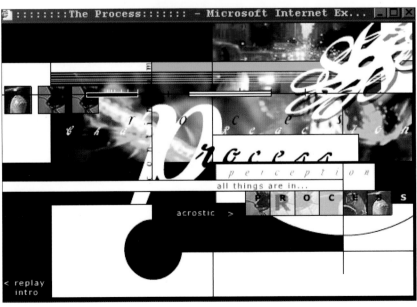

title
Timeticker
URL
www.timeticker.com/
Design firm
zwernemann
Designer
Martin zwernemann

This is an amusing little site that showcases the interactivity of Flash. There is no way that HTML could maintain the fluid motion that the Timeticker displays. As you scroll across the time zones, notice how evenly the highlights follow the mouse.

Bahamas / Nassau
Brazil / West Brazil **
Canada / Eastern Canada **
Cayman Islands / Georgetown
Colombia / Bogota

Australia / Sydney *
Australia / Victoria *
Austria / Vienna **
Azerbaijan / Baku **
Bahamas / Nassau

Timeticker is created by Martin Zwernemann (www

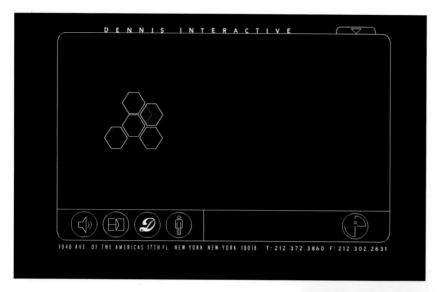

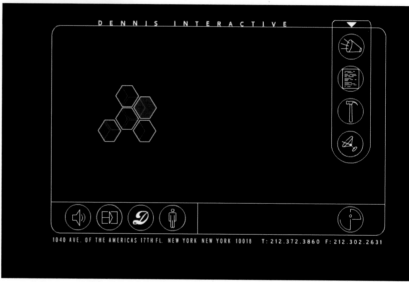

Title
Dennis Interactive
URL
www.dennisinter.com/di/disite.html
Design firm
Dennis publishing, Inc.

Here is a quick-loading, professional site that uses Flash animation to its fullest. Everything on this site moves. Each button is a separate, entertaining animation, but at no point does the interface confuse. The sound loop is short without becoming annoying. Because it is based on vector graphics, Flash is fully zoomable. In order to completely appreciate this site, zoom in on all the buttons; the animations look even better close up.

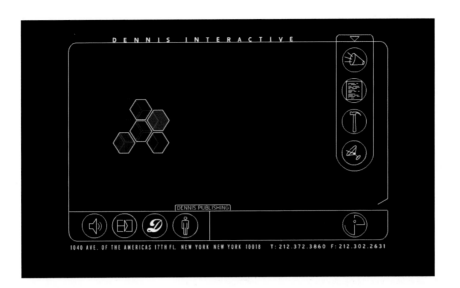

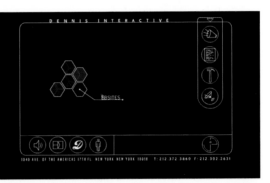

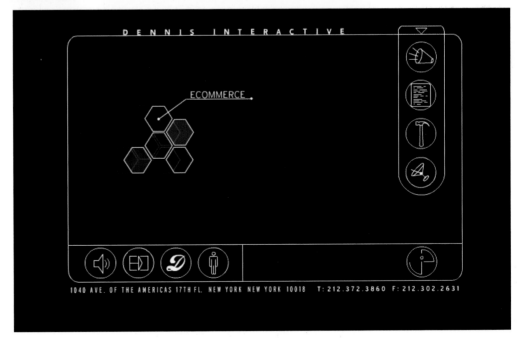

title
gobler toys
URL
www.goblertoys.com/
design firm
gobler toys
designer
steven casino

Gobler captures a fifties kitsch look. It is
one example of many sites on the Web
where design has turned back on itself due
to restrictions in color and speed that no
longer exist in print and other media. Gobler
works within these limitations to create a
compelling retro look. Gobler uses Flash to
make each banner a button as well.

title
   gobler toys
   URL
      www.goblertoys.com/
   design firm
      gobler toys
   designer
      steven casino

The "Fu Manchu, I Love You" animation continues the retro style in an imaginative, fun way. The download is a somewhat long (with a 56k modem), but the payoff is excellent. A funny "commercial" complete with music, voice-over, and moving pictures show the potential of Flash animation. When the world is wired with cable and high-speed modems, this could be the type of animation on every page.

title
wolvesburrow
URL
www.wolvesburrow.com/
Design firm
wolvesburrow

"What matters most is that we won't crash you," they say at Wolvesburrow. While this is true, their site is also a fun design. The colored stripes are a look rarely seen on the Internet and the buttons are easy to navigate and interesting to look at. In the "good news" section, there are a number of small Flash games to play, including a concentration game. All of these would have been extremely chunky, long downloads without the use of vector graphics. The entire site is fast-loading because of the use of simple, repeated images.

©1998, 1999, 2000 Wolvesburrow Productions - All Rights Reserved

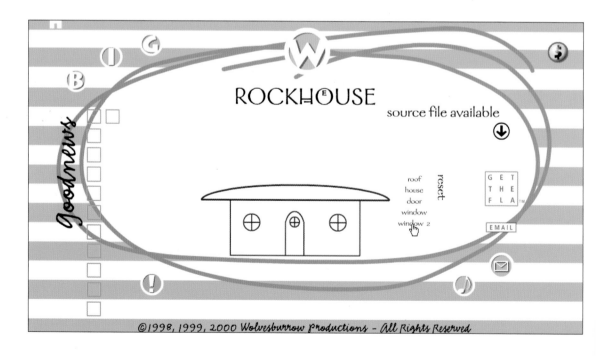

ROCKHOUSE
source file available

Goodnews

roof
house
door
window
window 2

reset

GET
THE
FLA™

EMAIL

©1998, 1999, 2000 Wolvesburrow Productions - All Rights Reserved

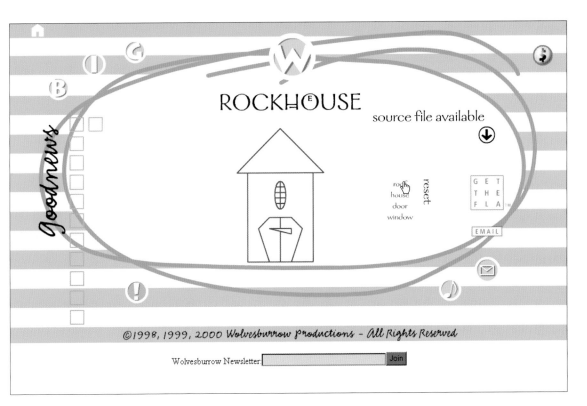

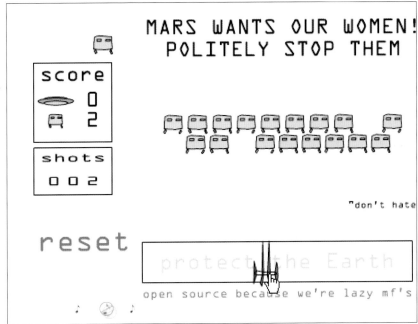

TITLE
Heavy.com
URL
www.heavy.com/
DESIGN FIRM
Heavy.com

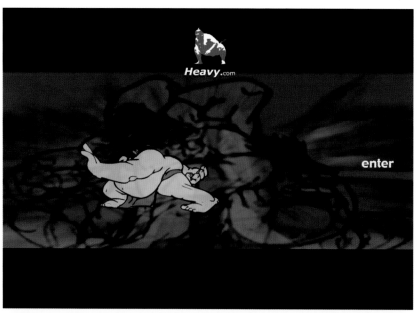

Heavy is one of the most exciting Fla
sites on the Internet. This site is uniqu
because they are willing to push the
boundaries. While large downloads ma
take some time for the immediate futu
Heavy has used Flash to minimize that ti
The result is a little bit of a wait but we
worth it. Streaming animations, trailers, a
short movies are all available to peruse. T
excellent illustrations give the site a cutting
edge look. Heavy.com has the type of cont
users will be seeking in the future.

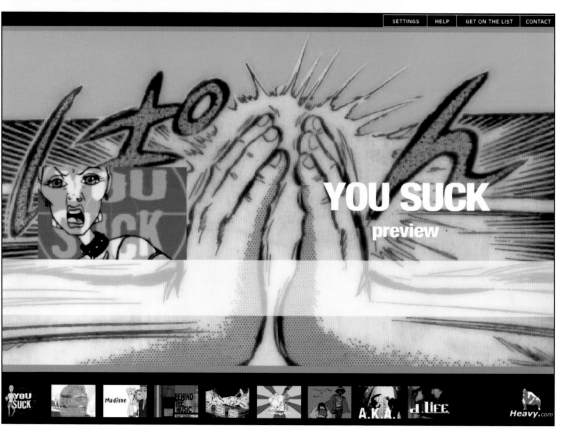

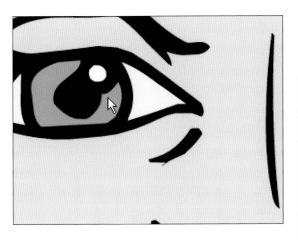

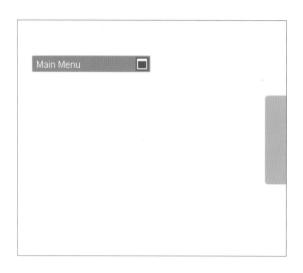

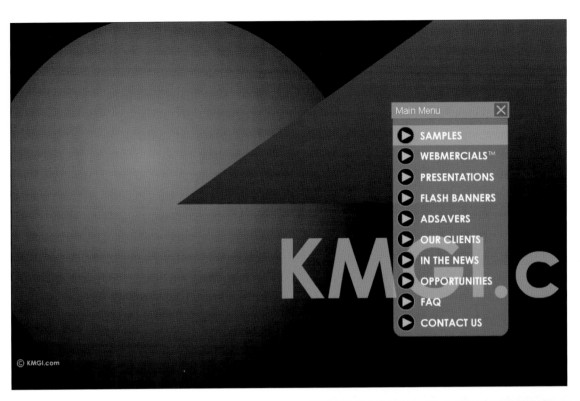

Title
KMGI
URL
www.kmgi.com/
Design Firm
KMGI.com Inc.

This is one of the first, if not the first Web site done entirely in Lingo, the Flash language. KMGI uses absolutely no HTML. Simple, iconic symbols repeat, minimizing download time while maintaining entertaining animation. One common problem with all Flash sites is the use of pseudo-frame boxes with a scroll bar that doesn't run smoothly up and down. KMGI solves this problem by loading the text in bite-size pieces with back and forth buttons. Check out the samples section for some beautiful movies that download in seconds.

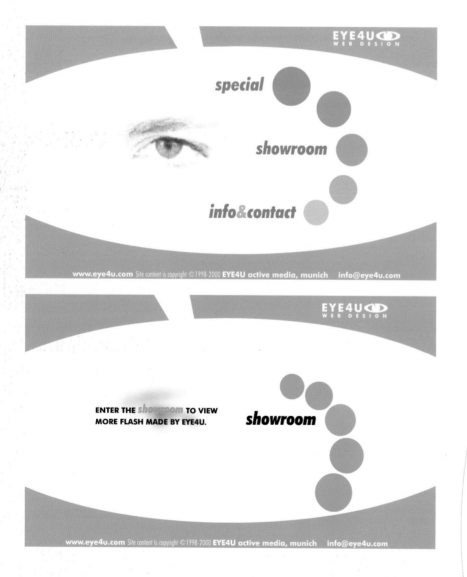

ENTER THE *showroom* **TO VIEW**
MORE FLASH MADE BY EYE4U.

TITLE
EYE4U
URL
eye4u.com/home/index.html
DESIGN FIRM
Eye 4 U Active Media

Making a site entertaining and interesting while keeping bandwidth down is a challenge for all Web designers. Eye4U credits their background in television production for keeping their focus squarely on low bandwidth. While the download time is short, the quantity of moving images and high-quality sound are truly stunning on this site. Check out the samples gallery for some interesting experiments that demonstrate just what Flash can do. The cubes-on-ice animation is amazing for its fluidity. Notice that there are only two actual images—the background and the cube. Changing the properties of the image creates the reflection of the cube.

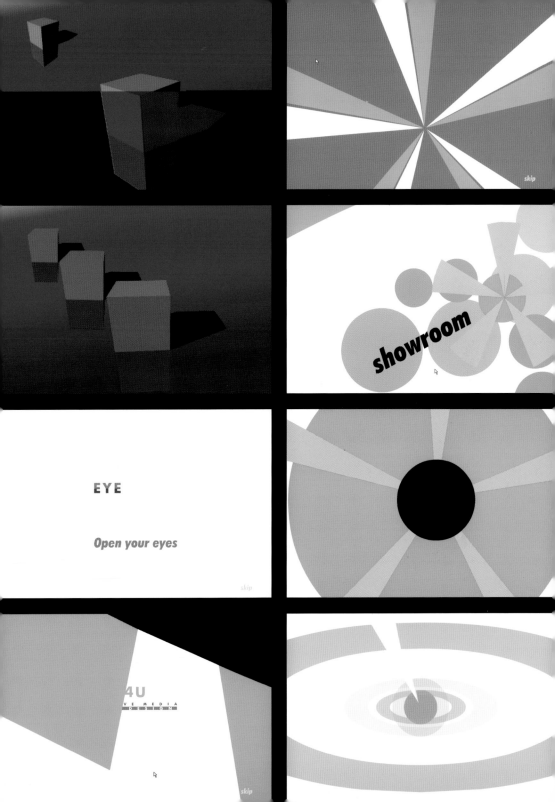

skip

showroom

EYE

Open your eyes

skip

4U
VE MEDIA
D I G N

skip

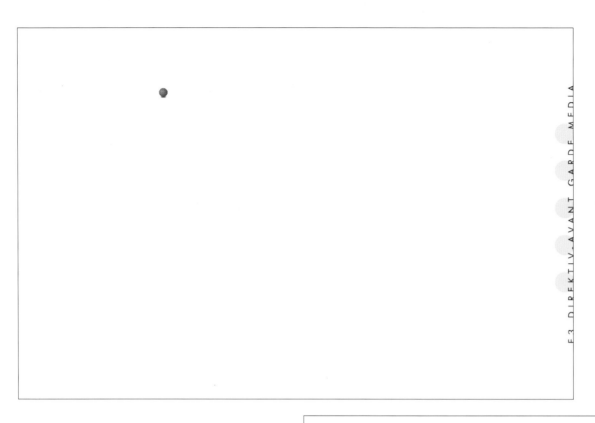

E3 DIREKTIV-AVANT GARDE MEDIA

E3 DIREKTIV-AVANT GARDE MEDIA

Title
E3 Directiv
URL
www.e3directive.com/
Design Firm
E3 Directiv
Designer
Fusion Media Group, Inc., Elmer Erana, producer

The opening Flash animation on this site is great. A ball comes "rolling" out and opens to disgorge smaller balls that become the navigation buttons. The hole is then covered with the E3 logo. A quick animation, this is another example of interesting design and animation done without sacrificing bandwidth.

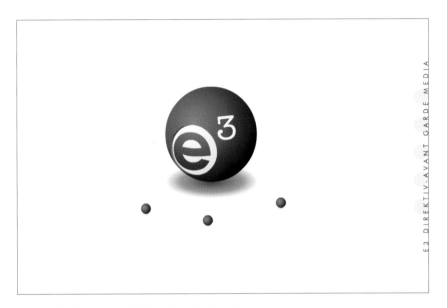

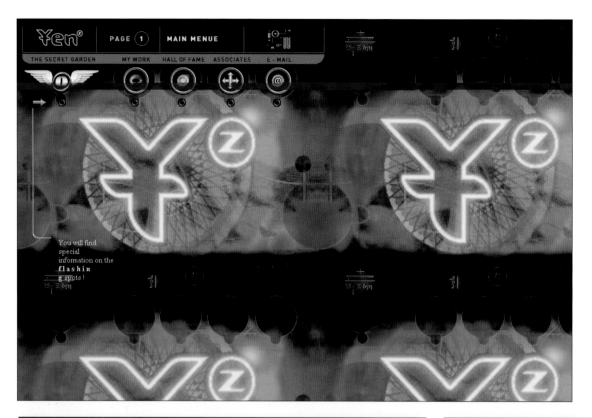

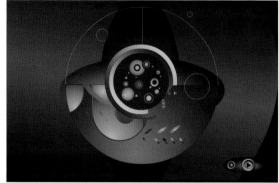

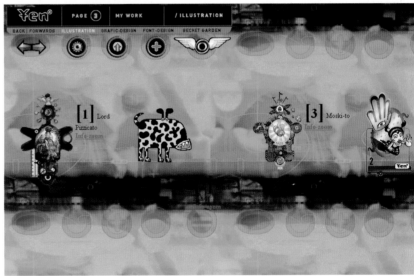

Title
Yenz
URL
www.yenz.com/
Design Firm
Yenz
Programmer
kosmokrator.com

Yenz is one of the more stunning and also odder sites on the Internet. The illustrations are excellent and the interactivity is impressive. In order to navigate this site, the user has to zoom in on areas to find the buttons in order to continue. Without giving away the fun of this site, the map of the "Secret Garden" shows there are over twenty possible steps to explore. In addition, there are at least three languages—Chinese, Japanese, and English—from this Italian designer's site.

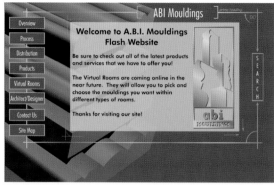

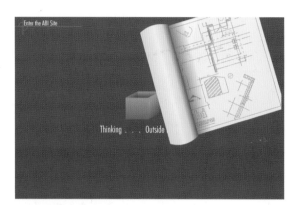

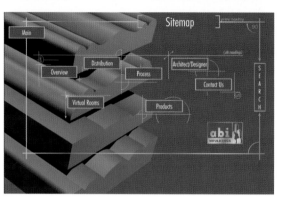

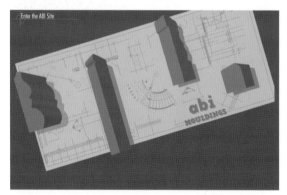

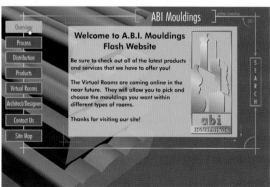

title
ABI Mouldings
URL
www.abimouldings.com/
Design Firm
ABI Mouldings

This site proves that Flash can even make mouldings exciting! The introduction that animates the ABI logo is excellent and uses the blueprint style to high effect. Check out the beautiful site map, which ironically is completely unnecessary on this well-planned site.

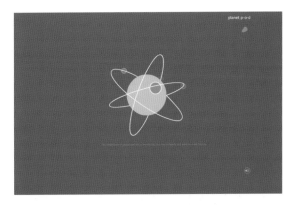

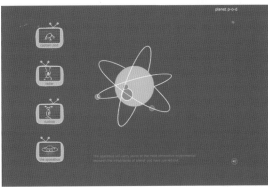

title
planet p-o-d
URL
www.p-o-d.co.uk/
design firm
pod new media ltd.

All aboard the space bus for planet p-o-d, a Flash-driven site inhabited by cute extra-terrestrials. Planet p-o-d features one of the best soundtracks on the Internet. While most sites stick with any easily loopable techno beat, p-o-d has a nice antique piano line that creates a counterpoint to the futuristic theme.

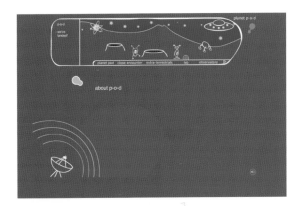

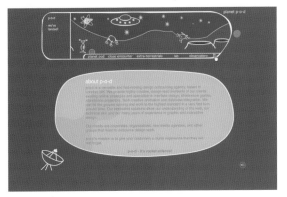

title
varazdin 2000
URL
www.2000.varazdin.com/
Design firm
varazdin

Varazdin is possibly the best Flash site on
the web. It is a map of Veljko, Sekelj's
hometown in Croatia. He is one of the first
true Flash designers; notice how the complete map uses no HTML. The interface
pops open to allow you to move around,
zoom in and out, turn the street names
off and on, and reveal the major build-
ings in town. Turn on the mini map to
jump around to different areas.

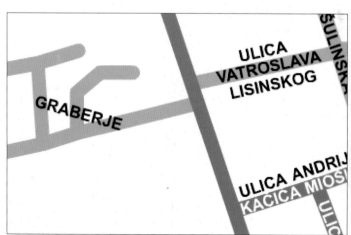

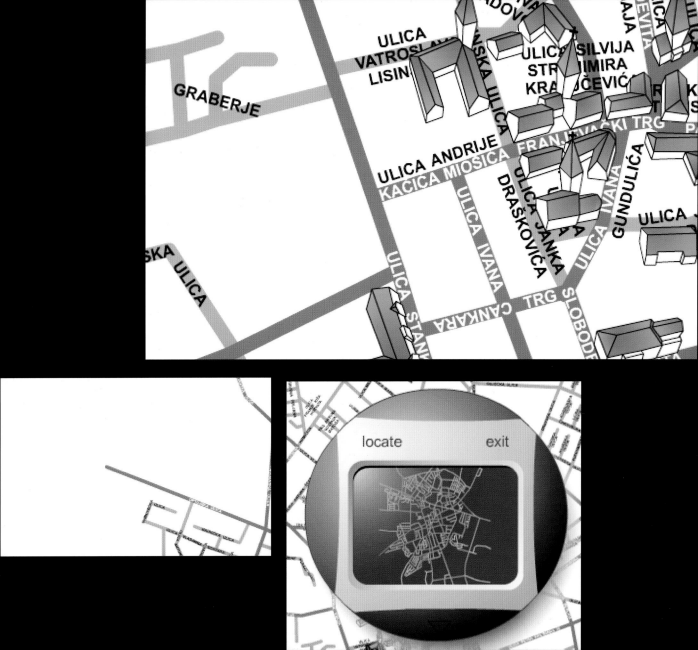

title
typographic
URL
www.typographic.com/
Design firm
typographic
Designer
jimmy chen

Typographic stays true to their name by
doing interesting and Flash-y things with
their typefaces. Letters seem to fly everywhere,
but the essential information, such as where
the links are, is clear and concise.

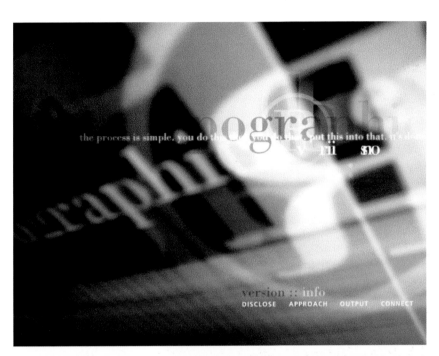

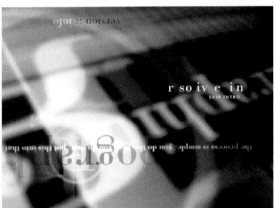

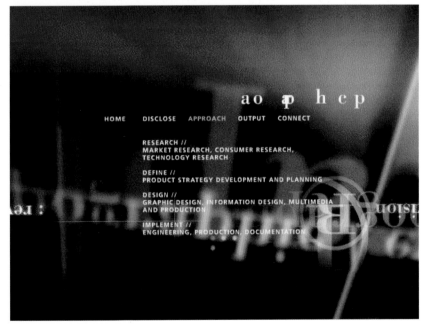

title
Dirk Rullkötter AGD
url
www.rullkoetter.de/
design firm
Rullkötter AGD werbung + design

A bee follows the cursor around the page with a disturbingly realistic sound effect. The little bee is a great example of the possibilities of Flash on the Internet. Because it is one image, it takes moments for the image to load, and movement to bandwidth is almost limitless using vector graphics.

Title
Ricochet
URL
www.ricochetcreativethinking.co/
Design Firm
Ricochet Creative Thinking
Designers
Nicholas Henry, Steve Zelle

The opening animation on the Ricochet site draws you immediately into what they are all about. Multi-colored blocks move around the grid until they get into the right order, like the old children's puzzle. Creative thinking is the point.

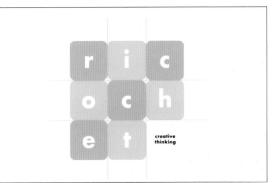

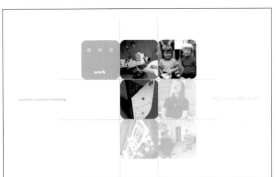

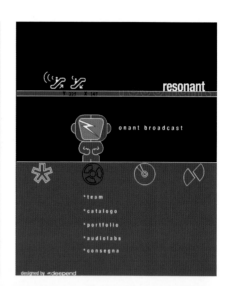

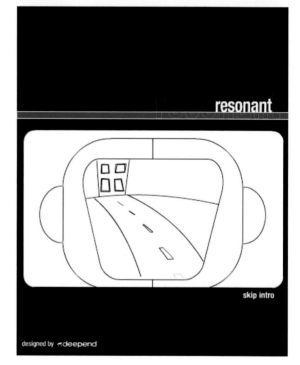

title
resonant
URL
www.resonant.it/
design firm
resonant srl

A fun animation introduces you to the
Resonant alien quickly and amusingly.
Once inside, the alien follows the cursor
back and forth over the buttons. The site
loads quickly because the alien image loads
into your cache right at the beginning.

title
ragingPixels
URL
*www.regingpixels.com/flash/
regingpixels.html*
Design Firm
Raging Pixels

"Where art and technology meet,"
ragingPixels is a great Flash site. The
buttons are animated nicely. The page
also scrolls left to right, instead of up
and down, a unique design touch.

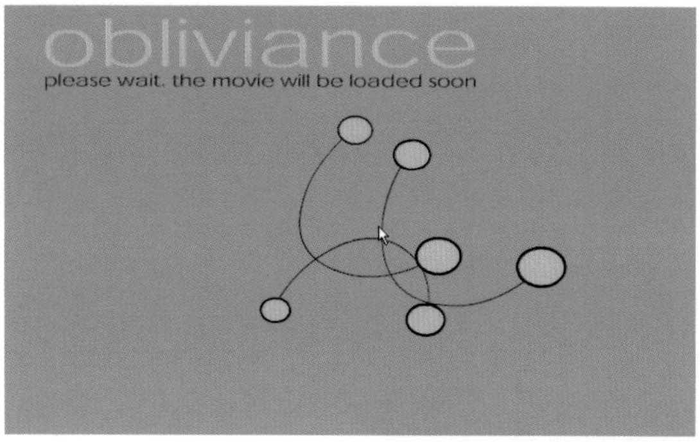

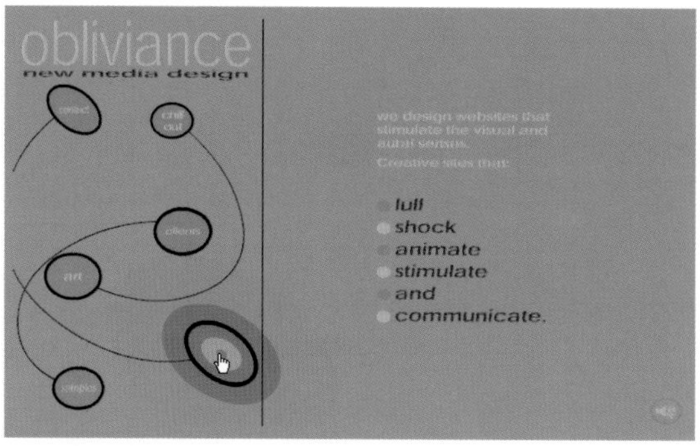

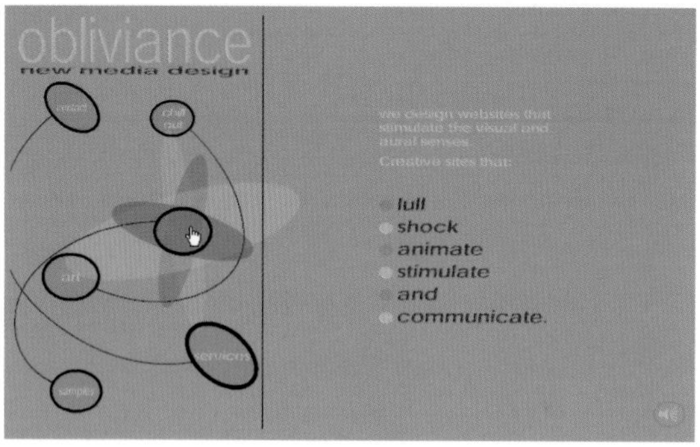

Title
obliviance
URL
www.obliviance.ndirect.co.uk/
Design Firm
obliviance
Designer
Rosalind Miller

The loading screen at Obliviance moves almost like a kinetic sculpture. The simple animation becomes the interface, six buttons that move. This is a great example of a site that, if it were even possible, would take forever to load in HTML.

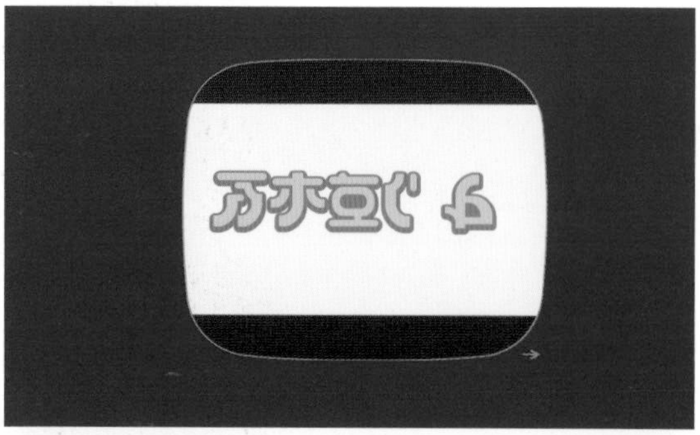

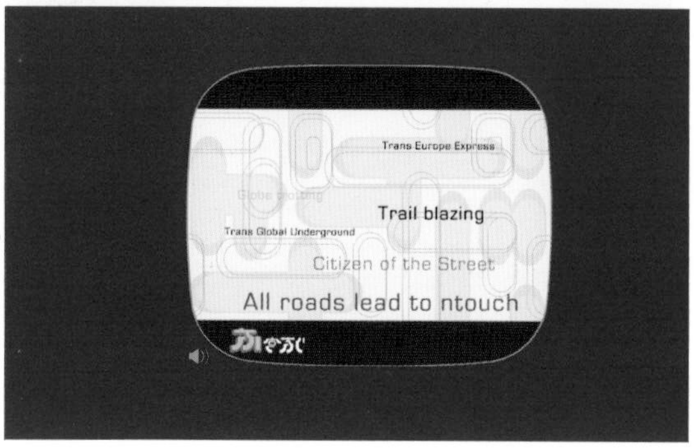

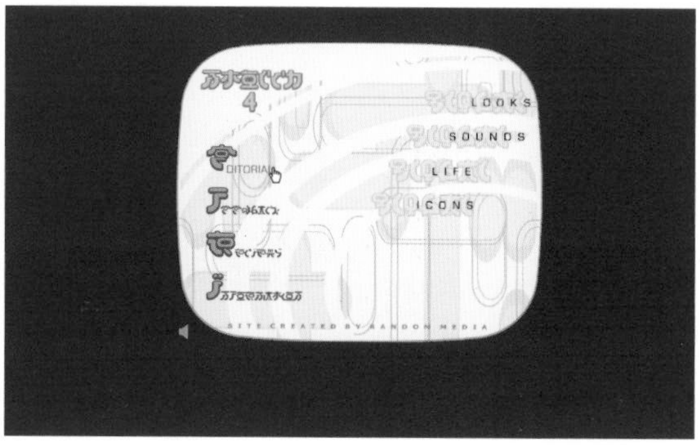

title
ntouch
URL
ntouch.linst.ac.uk/
design firm
Random Media

The creative use of Flash on this site lies in the sound. Weird sound effects come together into a fun disco beat. Each button is an animated word in Chinese that fades to reveal English text underneath.

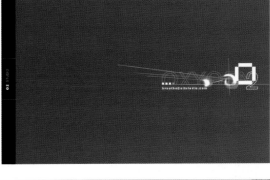

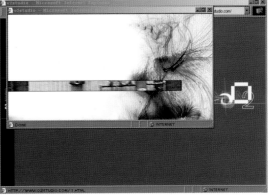

title
o2 studios
URL
www.o2studios.com/
design firm
o2 studios

Jarring images and unexplained buttons are not a bad thing at this site. O2 Studios is one of the few true art sites on the Internet. Flash allows each button to lead to its own short, self-contained movie.

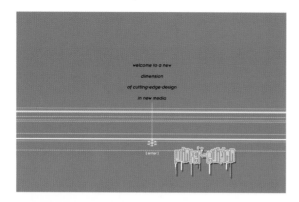

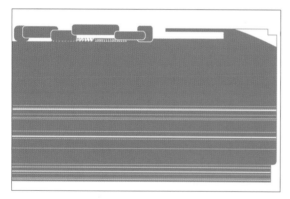

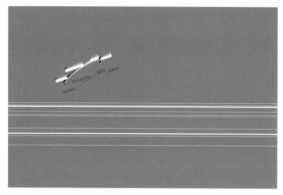

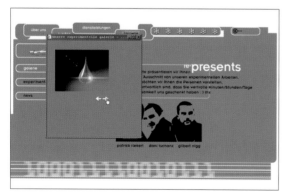

title
netgraphic
URL
www.netgraphic.ch/
Design firm
audiobox ulanghanzepte

The interface flies out of the corner, casting a shadow as it moves. This design highlights how Flash can be used to create simple, three-dimensional effects. The shadow is the same image as the interface with the color changed.

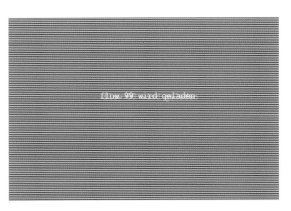

title
wojtek
URL
www.wojtek.de/
design firm
perplex GMBH
designer
sal wojtek

An online comic, Wojtek uses some effects that are rarely seen on the Internet. The rotating interface takes a moment to figure out, but it is a neat way to navigate the site. The remarkable loading screen grabs your attention right away with a television-static effect.

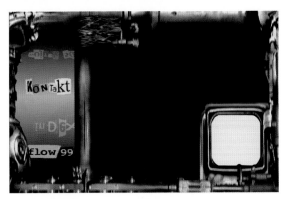

title
The Multimedia Group
URL
www.themmgroup.com/
Design Firm
The Multimedia Group

The Multimedia Group is one of the new breed of fun Flash sites. There's a lot going on here. Images and text fly around the screen during the introduction; everything appears in a very natural manner. The opening animation is somewhat busy but not to the point of confusion.

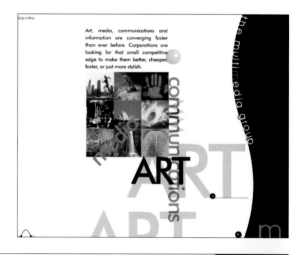

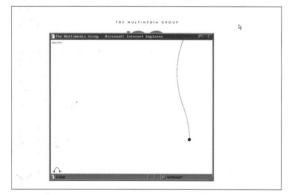

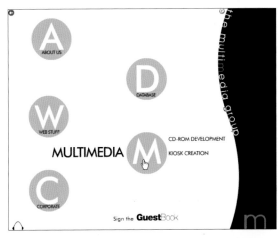

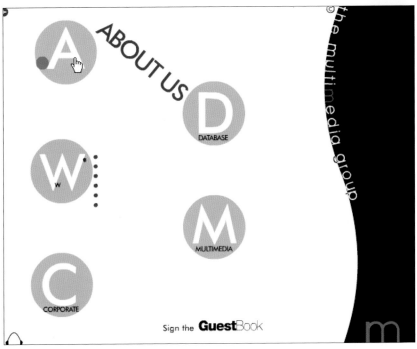

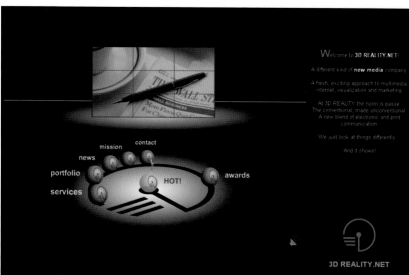

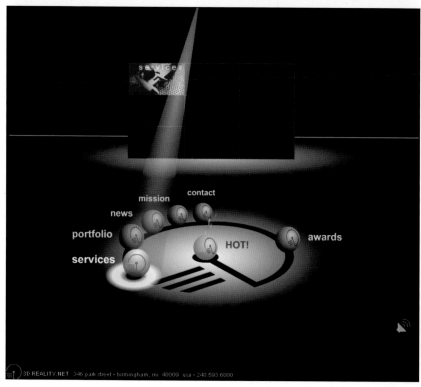

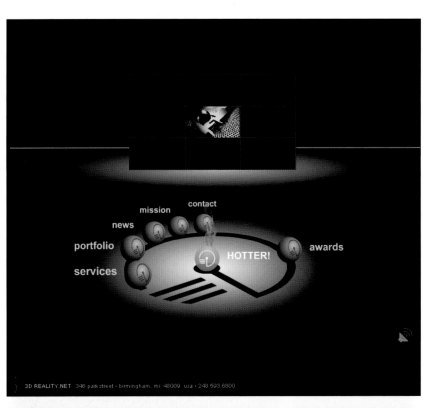

title
3D Reality
URL
www.3dreality.net/main.html
Design firm
3D Reality
Designers
Les Fram, R. Tyler smith

3D Reality uses a Flash animation within a frame to great effect. The opening animation is excellent, and the sound is among the best on the Internet. The main page has impressive effects on mouse-over, like the "hot" button becoming "hotter," and spotlights too.

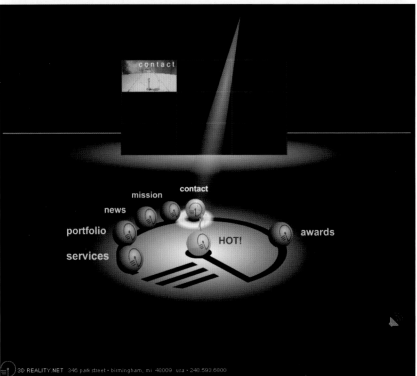

title
Jon Duarte communications
URL
www.jonduarte.com/
Design firm
Jon Duarte communications

Jon Duarte uses the pop-up window to great effect, making the animation large enough to cover the lower windows, without using the entire screen's real estate. Flash-enabled buttons enhance the modern design. On mouse-over, text and shapes fall toward the buttons. Subtle geometric shapes move constantly in the background.

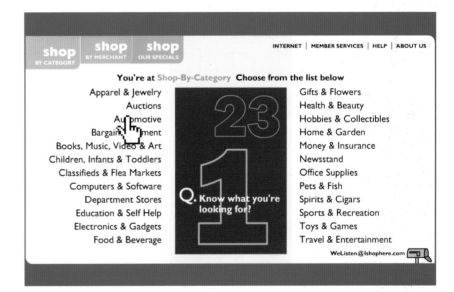

TITLE
I SHOP HERE
URL
www.ishophere.com/
DESIGN FIRM
Ishophere.com

Even e-commerce can use vector graphics and animations. The I Shop Here site uses a Flash window as sort of revolving billboard to point to all their products and contests. The effect is not much different from a .gif image, but the .gif could show only two or three repeating images, whereas the Flash window can play virtually unlimited simple images.

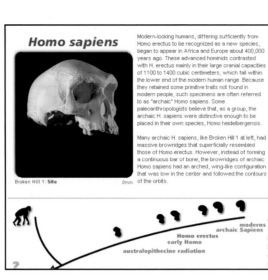

Homo sapiens

Modern-looking humans, differing sufficiently from Homo erectus to be recognized as a new species, began to appear in Africa and Europe about 400,000 years ago. These advanced hominids contrasted with H. erectus mainly in their large cranial capacities of 1100 to 1400 cubic centimeters, which fall within the lower end of the modern human range. Because they retained some primitive traits not found in modern people, such specimens are often referred to as "archaic" Homo sapiens. Some paleoanthropologists believe that, as a group, the archaic H. sapiens were distinctive enough to be placed in their own species, Homo heidelbergensis.

Many archaic H. sapiens, like Broken Hill 1 at left, had massive browridges that superficially resembled those of Homo erectus. However, instead of forming a continuous bar of bone, the browridges of archaic Homo sapiens had an arched, wing-like configuration that was low in the center and followed the contours of the orbits.

Broken Hill 1: **Site**   0mm

moderns — 0
archaic Sapiens — 1
Homo erectus — 2
early Homo — 3
australopithecine radiation — 4
— 5

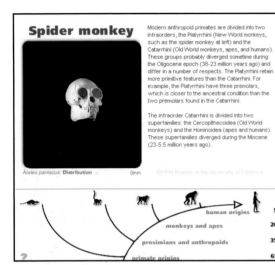

Spider monkey

Modern anthropoid primates are divided into two infraorders, the Platyrrhini (New World monkeys, such as the spider monkey at left) and the Catarrhini (Old World monkeys, apes, and humans). These groups probably diverged sometime during the Oligocene epoch (38-23 million years ago) and differ in a number of respects. The Platyrrhini retain more primitive features than the Catarrhini. For example, the Platyrrhini have three premolars, which is closer to the ancestral condition than the two premolars found in the Catarrhini.

The infraorder Catarrhini is divided into two superfamilies: the Cercopithecoidea (Old World monkeys) and the Hominoidea (apes and humans). These superfamilies diverged during the Miocene (23-5.5 million years ago).

Ateles paniscus: **Distribution**   0mm   ©1998 Regents of the University of California

human origins — 5
monkeys and apes — 20
prosimians and anthropoids — 35
primate origins — 65

Spider monkey

Modern anthropoid primates are divided into two infraorders, the Platyrrhini (New World monkeys, such as the spider monkey at left) and the Catarrhini (Old World monkeys, apes, and humans). These groups probably diverged sometime during the Oligocene epoch (38-23 million years ago) and differ in a number of respects. The Platyrrhini retain more primitive features than the Catarrhini. For example, the Platyrrhini have three premolars, which is closer to the ancestral condition than the two premolars found in the Catarrhini.

The infraorder Catarrhini is divided into two superfamilies: the Cercopithecoidea (Old World monkeys) and the Hominoidea (apes and humans). These superfamilies diverged during the Miocene (23-5.5 million years ago).

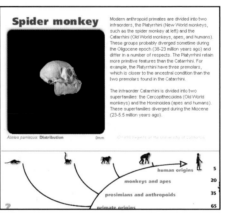

Ateles paniscus: **Distribution**   0mm   ©1998 Regents of the University of California

human origins — 5
monkeys and apes — 20
prosimians and anthropoids — 35
primate origins — 65

Homo sapiens

Modern-looking humans, differing sufficiently from Homo erectus to be recognized as a new species, began to appear in Africa and Europe about 400,000 years ago. These advanced hominids contrasted with H. erectus mainly in their large cranial capacities of 1100 to 1400 cubic centimeters, which fall within the lower end of the modern human range. Because they retained some primitive traits not found in modern people, such specimens are often referred to as "archaic" Homo sapiens. Some paleoanthropologists believe that, as a group, the archaic H. sapiens were distinctive enough to be placed in their own species, Homo heidelbergensis.

Many archaic H. sapiens, like Broken Hill 1 at left, had massive browridges that superficially resembled those of Homo erectus. However, instead of forming a continuous bar of bone, the browridges of archaic Homo sapiens had an arched, wing-like configuration that was low in the center and followed the contours of the orbits.

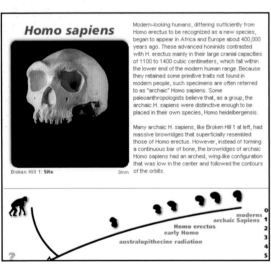

Broken Hill 1: **Site**   0mm

moderns — 0
archaic Sapiens — 1
Homo erectus — 2
early Homo — 3
australopithecine radiation — 4
— 5

title
Human Evolution
URL
www.sscf.ucsb.edu/~hagen/crania
Designers
phillip L. walker, Edward H. Hagen, Dirk Brandts University of california, santa Barbara, Department of Anthropology

The primate skulls can be rotated 360 degrees, giving a real sense of structure and weight. There are sixteen separate images in the animation. This is exactly the type of animation that would be possible, but improbable because of its size, without Flash.

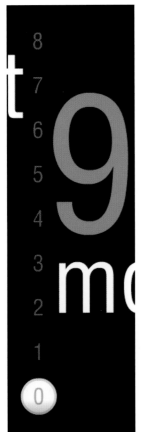

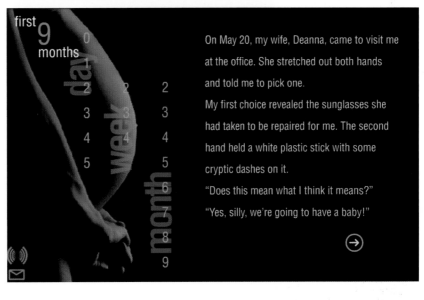

On May 20, my wife, Deanna, came to visit me at the office. She stretched out both hands and told me to pick one.

My first choice revealed the sunglasses she had taken to be repaired for me. The second hand held a white plastic stick with some cryptic dashes on it.

"Does this mean what I think it means?"

"Yes, silly, we're going to have a baby!"

title
first 9 months
URL
www.first9months.com/
Design firm
12 south.com
Designer
Joseph Moore

Take a virtual journey through the first nine months of a baby's life, with a great soundtrack. First 9 Months turns their back on the common techno loop. A quiet guitar serenades the viewer and fits nicely with the content. The next time you have a spare half hour, investigate this site.

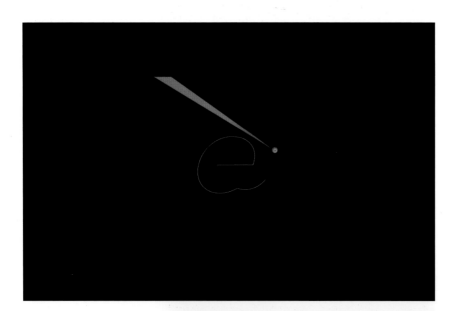

title
Eurorunner
URL
www.eurorunner.com/
design firm
Euro.runner srl
designers
Jacopo Deyla/flash, Giuseppe
Covino/Art Director, Franco
Milazzo/Technical/

Check out the opening animation. A laser burns the e logo into the blackness and four pipes protrude, separating the buttons. On mouse-over, a gunfight icon follows the cursor

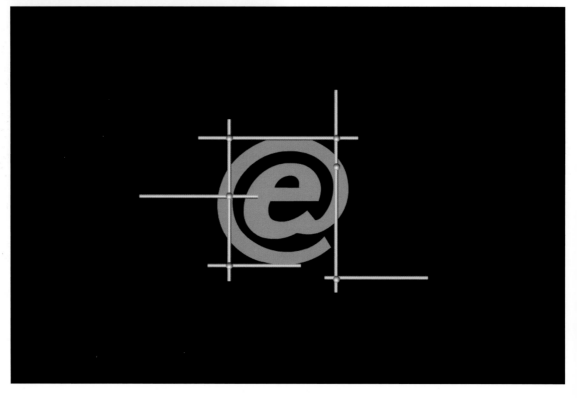

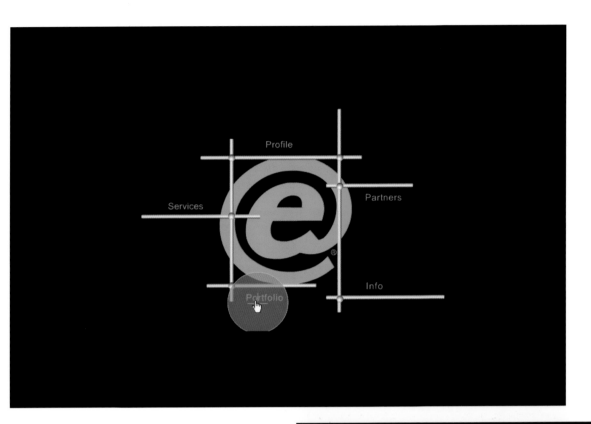

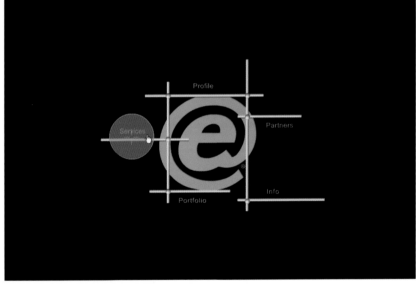

title
D+CON/trol
URL
www.decontrol.com/deconv1/
Design Firm
One Ten Design Inc.

D+CON/trol is a site that uses a Flash pop-up window. This high-concept site has impressive interactivity due to the use of Flash. Every button is animated nicely, although there is no hint as to where those buttons will lead you.

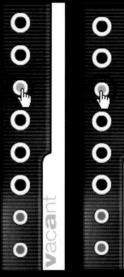

D+CON TROL

¿WHAT'S THE DEAL?

--**D+CON/trol**-- is an experimental exercise in the loss of viewer control over the developing web medium. Web users, weary to lose valuable time and waste precious energy, have become information scavengers clicking endlessly in search of vital information yet invariably failing to perceive their on-line environment in the process. --**D+CON/trol**-- explores this by manipulating viewer response to content that is normally provided through linked visual guideposts to information. Disoriented and removed from the rat race of normal web browsing, the viewer of -- **D+CON/trol**-- is unknowingly assimilated into a landscape of seemingly

title
4 Guys
URL
www.4guys.com/
Design Firm
4 Guys Interactive

The 4 Guys site combines Flash and frames into
extremely usable site. The Flash animation keep
this site visually interesting, while the frames c
nize an impressive amount of information inte
usable format.

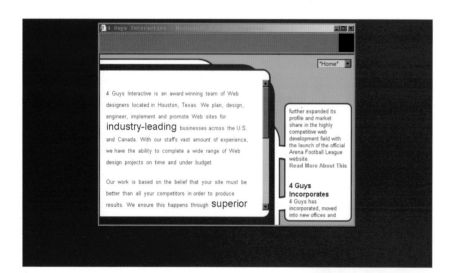

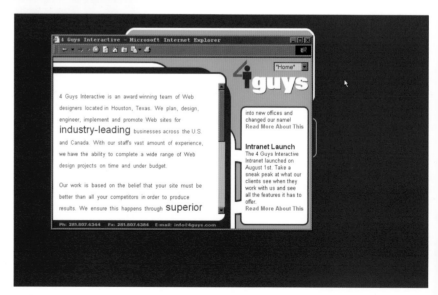

<Skip this introduction>

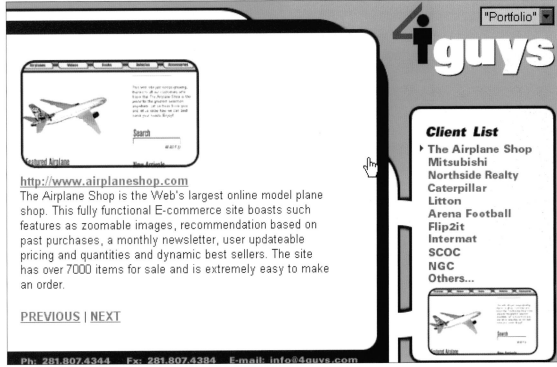

title
online interview with Randall Larson
URL
people.mn.mediaone.net/gonzoz
design firm
online interview with Randall Larson

The use of Flash makes everything on this page a button. Randall Larson can't draw very well, so he makes everything light up and move. Although the illustrations are interesting, the interactivity is awesome. Stars follow the cursor around the screen but they can be turned off, if you prefer.

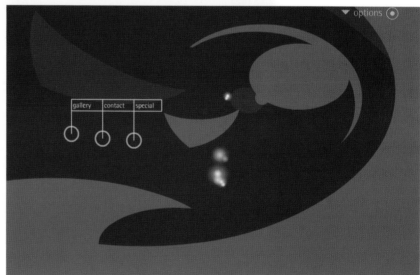

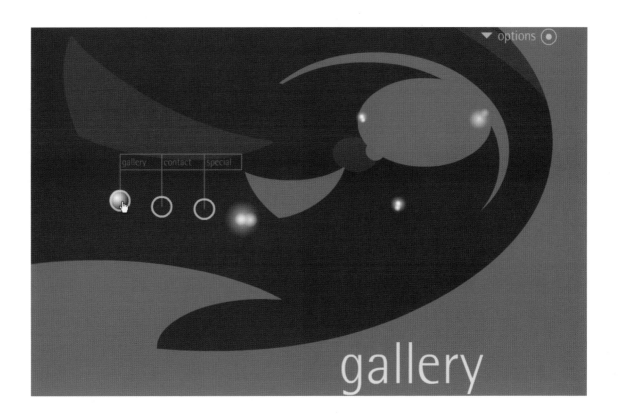

title
Asmussen interactive
URL
turtleshell.com/asm

The futuristic look of this site is incredible.
The simple, iconic image of the painter's hand
in the corner leading into the site is elegant. The
balls of light create some simple motion to keep
the viewer's attention. The sound on this site is
among the best on the Internet.

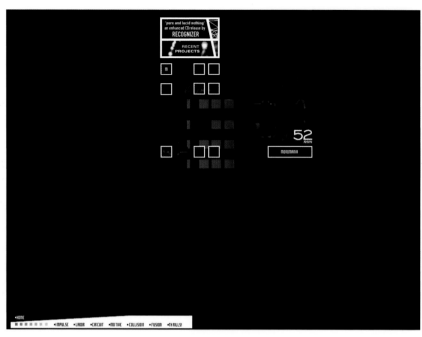

Title
52 mm
URL
www.52mm.com/
Design Firm
52 mm

52 mm is a site that falls into the art-for-art's-sake category. The navigation is somewhat ambiguous, and the images don't always make total sense. Still, the overall design works.

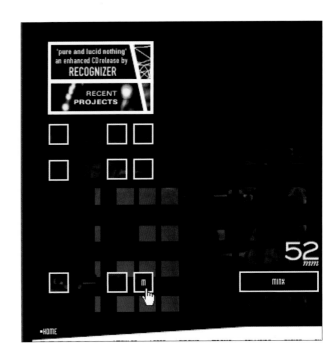

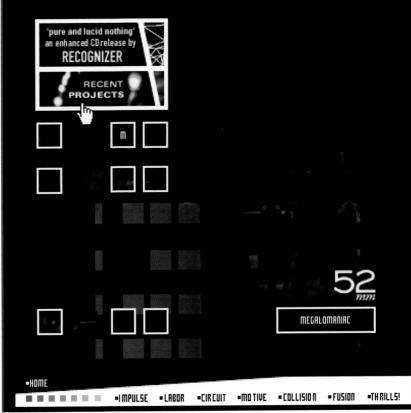

title
DDBunch
URL
www.ddbunch.com/
design firm
Diciamo Digital Buch SRL

On every page, DDBunch uses their interesting logo illustration. The transitions between the pages are smooth, and repeating the same image cuts down on download time, as it is loaded into your cache the first time you view it.

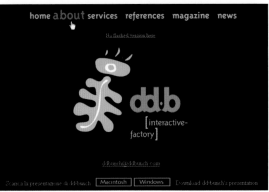

It's <u>BIG</u> and it's loading
Loading status: 2%

melon.

Title
Melon Dezign
URL
www.melondezign.com/
Design Firm
Melon Dezign

Great illustrations move in an art-for-art's-sake site. They are honest with you right up front with the "It's big and it's loading screen," which does take a while to load. Melon does keep you entertained though, with a series of iconic images to click through. Once inside, the somewhat disturbing images spin and dance around the multicolored screens. Melon is truly pushing the envelope of what is possible in Web design.

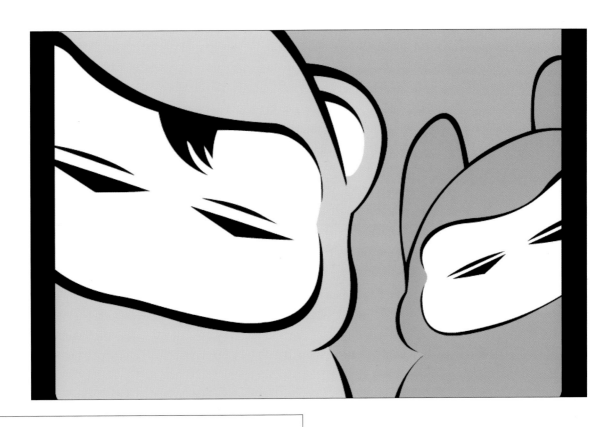

It's **BIG** and it's loading
Loading status: 3%

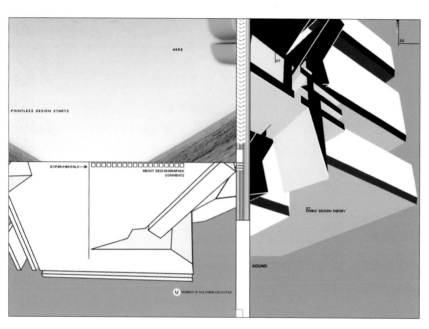

TITLE
Designgraphik
URL
www.designgraphik.com/
DESIGN FIRM
Designgraphik
DESIGNER
Mike Young

Designgraphik is an experimental site that features self-described pointless design that spins and dances before you. All Flash enhanced, the site is ambiguous in its navigation, but for this site, that's the point. This site stands refreshingly alone on the Internet as one that is not trying to sell anything.

HERE

1. POINTLESS DESIGN STARTS

THANKS. EPYT.

ANSWERS
I WORK FOR VIR2L, THAT WOULD PROBABLY EXPLAIN ANY SIMILARITIES.
I DO INTERACTIVE SHIT ALL DAY LONG AT WORK.
I ALREADY LEARNED FLASH.
YES, THE TEXT IS SMALL.

ex·per·i·men·tal (k-spr mntl)
adj. Abbr. exp., exptl., X, x Relating to or based on
experiment: experimental procedures;
experimental results. Given to experimenting. Of
the nature of an experiment; constituting or
undergoing a test: an experimental drug.
Founded on experience; empirical.

SOUND

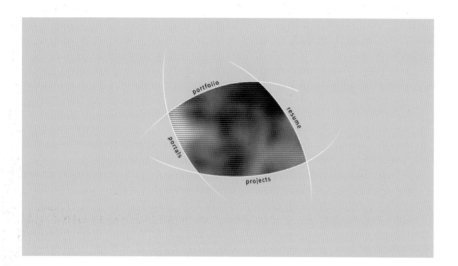

Title
Andy Lim
URL
andy.artdirectors.com/
Design firm
Embedded wireless labs

The interface on this site is excellent, with a good number of images but not enough to necessitate a long download. The other pages also have great animations and easy interactivity. The overall look of this site is great; the colors and images are subdued and easy to view.

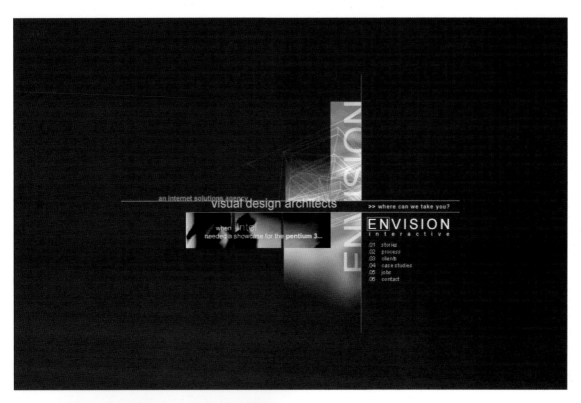

Title
Envision Interactive
URL
www.envisioninteractive.com/
Design Firm
Envision Interactive

"It was important to achieve two objectives: Keep bandwidth down and create a sense of motion," says Envision president Spencer Lum. Both objectives are realized brilliantly. The centerpiece of the site, the three panels in the middle, use a single image that is manipulated using fades and resizing in Flash.

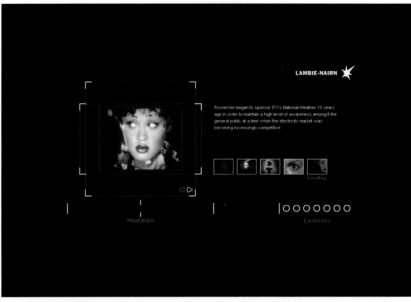

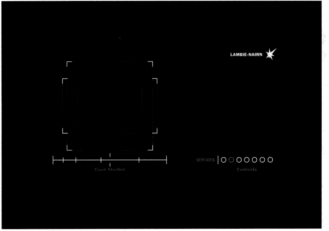

TITLE
Lambie-Nairn

URL
www.lambie-nairn.com/flash_go.html

DESIGN FIRM
Lambie-Nairn

This Lambie-Nairn site has one of the best Flash interfaces. Click on one of the buttons along the right side; the box slides open over the button to reveal the information you requested. Click on the slide bar below the box to view the images of Lambie-Nairn's work.

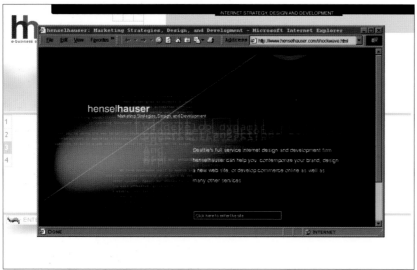

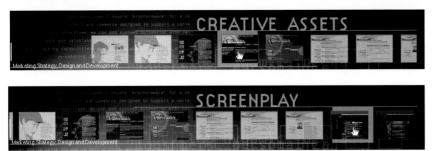

Title
Hensel Hauser
URL
www.henselhauser.com/
Design Firm
Hensel Hauser
Designer
Todd Hauser

Hensel Hauser is an impressively easy site to navigate, particularly with the extensive use of Flash. The new types of interfaces work extremely naturally and the traditional ones are truly traditional. The nontraditional interfaces include the design examples that feature thumbnails in a row. The thumbnails actually move in response to your cursor and highlight on mouse-over. Click on the image to enlarge.

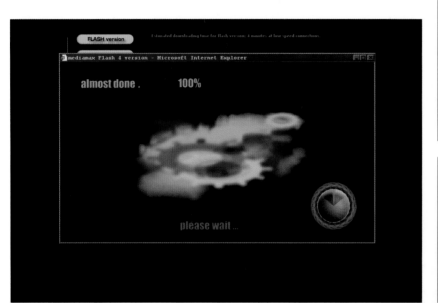

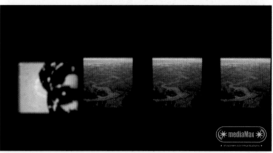

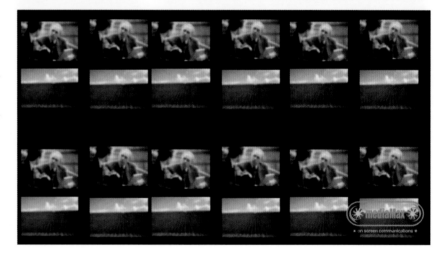

TITLE
mediamax

URL
www.mediamax.gr

DESIGN FIRM
mediamax

This is one of the most extensive Flash sites on the Internet. The opening animation features various photos panning and resizing all over the screen. The interface takes a little getting used to but it's great once you get used to where you are supposed to click.

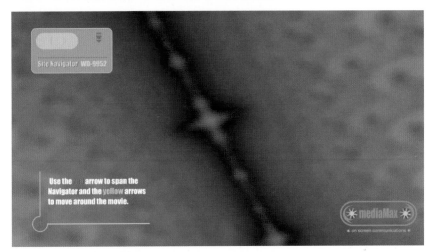

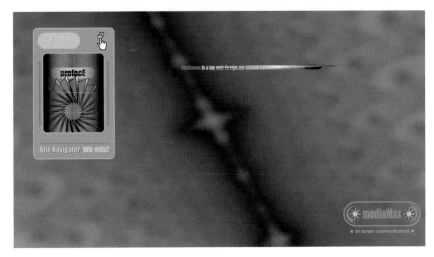

Title
MKsite
URL
mksite.com/
Design firm
MKsite
Designer
Massimo Kunstler

The MKSite uses Flash to great effect, particularly on the main interface where you scroll over the buttons and excellent iconic images pan in from the side. The opening animation is well worth the time.

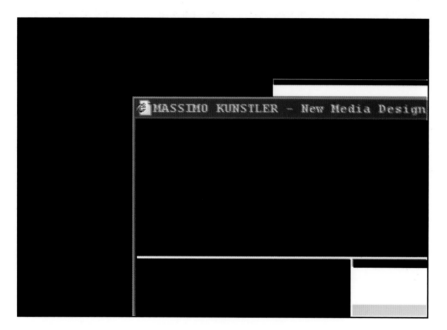

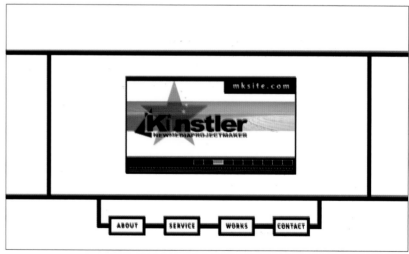

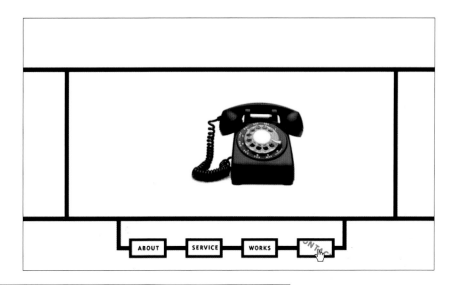

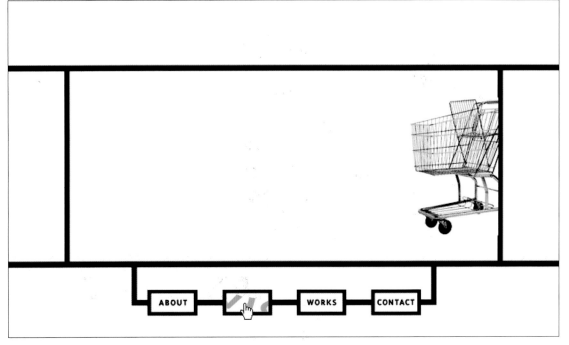

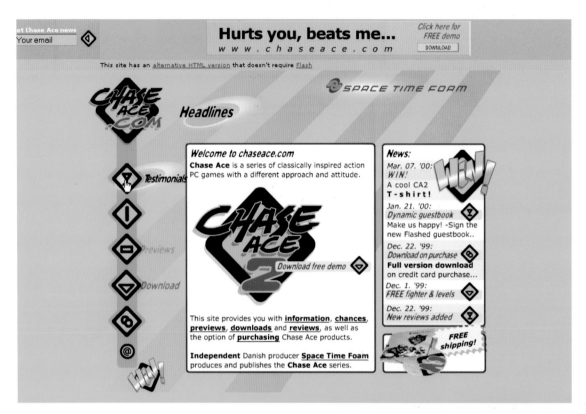

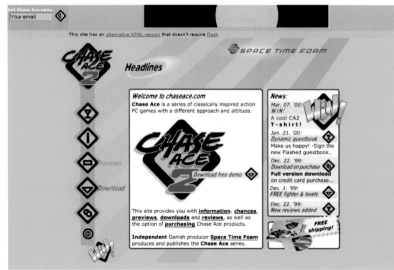

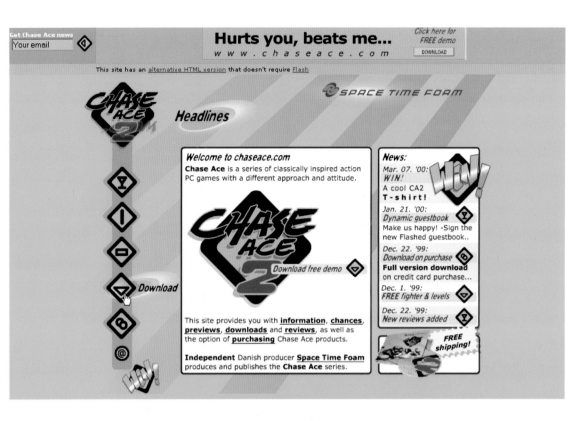

Title
chase ace

URL
www.chaseace.com/

Design firm
petergrafik/space time foam

Designer
peter holm

The Chase Ace site uses bright colors and
lots of movement to grab your attention
and hold it. A street-sign design works well
with the overall concept, and the interface
features text that scrolls quickly by until
mouse-over, when the text solidifies.

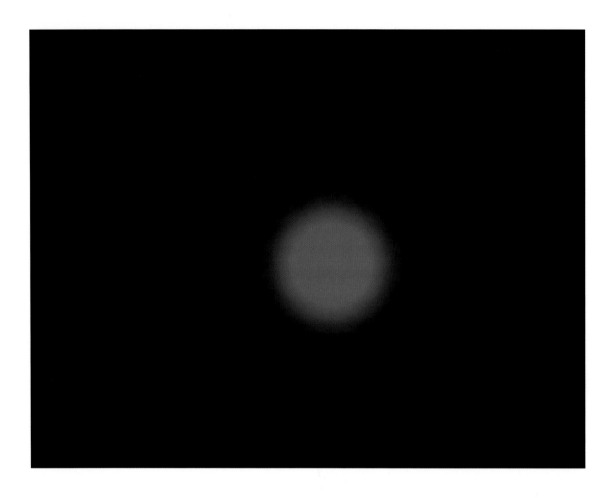

title
Hyper-Active
URL
www.bsimedia.com/
Design firm
BSI Media

The Hyper-Active site is a great example
of how Flash can be used simply to create
neat effects that wouldn't be possible with
HTML. Even this relatively basic (and
therefore fast-loading) site is compelling
due to the moving interface.

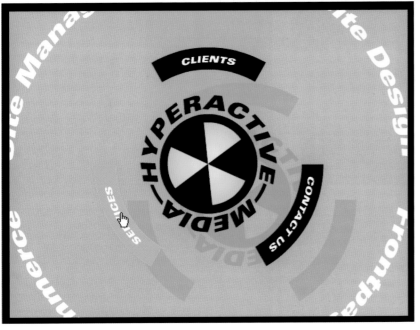

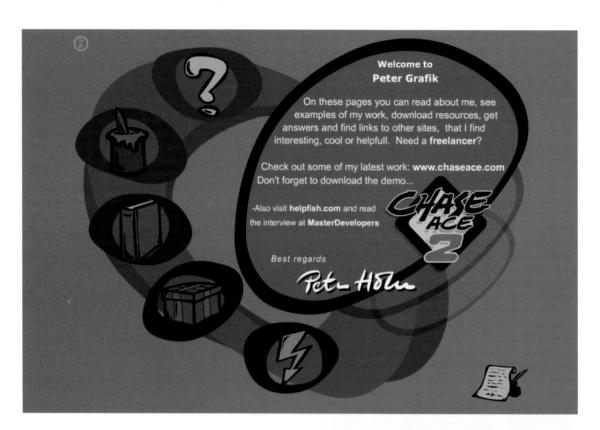

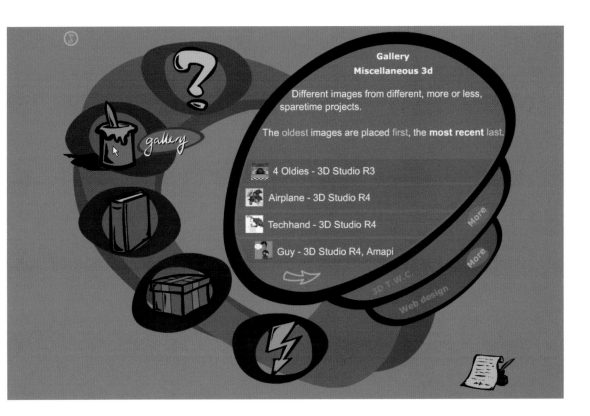

Title
petergrafik
URL
www.petergrafik.dk/
Design Firm
petergrafik/space time foam

Petergrafik uses Flash to make awesome animated
buttons. On mouse-over, the illustrations pop up over
the buttons. Once clicked, the information loads
into the blob to the right of the buttons. The browns
are also a nice contrast to the usual Web palette.

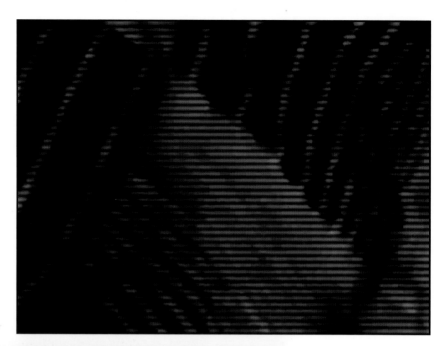

Title
mobley media
URL
www.mobleymedia.com/
Design firm
mobley media
Designer
margie mobley

The moving pictures draw you into this site immediately, and the fantastic illustrations keep your attention. Mobley Media uses color to great effect as well. One of the often over-looked features of Flash is the versatile color editor and its ability to import colors from Photoshop, .gifs, or even other Web pages.

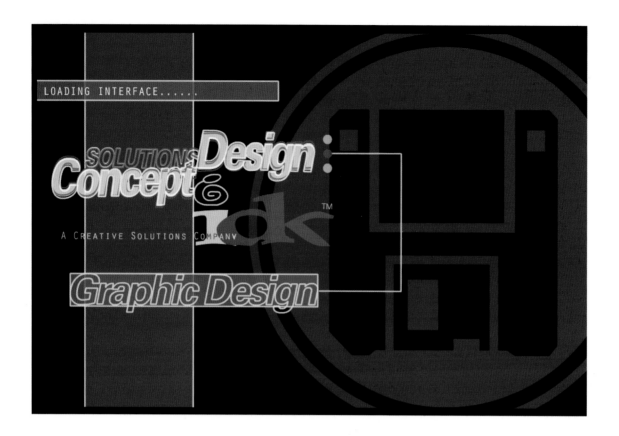

title
iconiklastique
URL
www.ida-a-ok.com/
Design firm
iconiklastique Design Klinik, LLC

The interface is excellent on this site. The buttons become the main image for the background after you click on them. This is a great idea for vector graphics, considering its ability to zoom in forever. Once the image is loaded, Flash allows you to play with it any way you would like.

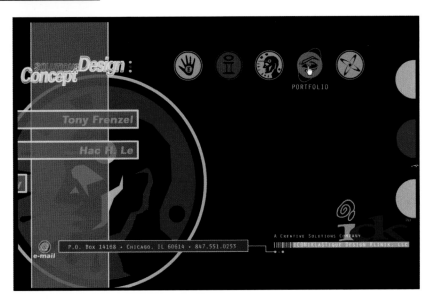

Title
insomnious
URL
www.insomnious.com/
Design firm
insomnious, Ltd.

At Insomnious, they have designed one of the most creative sites on the web. The interface takes a moment to get used to but increases the interactivity of the site. You can move the information boxes anywhere you would like on the screen. You can choose among four backgrounds.

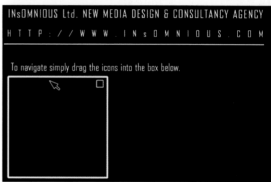

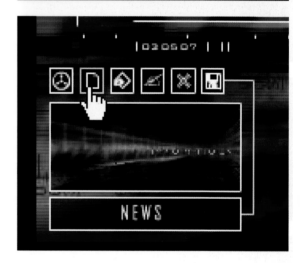

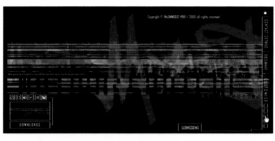

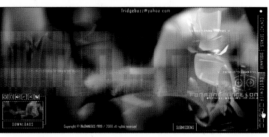

ALL DESIGNERS WORLDWIDE ARE WELCOME TO SUBMIT
BACKGROUNDS FOR THIS SITE. ONE DESIGNERS
BACKGROUND WILL BE FEAUTERED PER MONTH.
THE IMAGE MUST BE 800 BY 360 PIXELS.

SUBMISSIONS   MAIL THE SUBMISSION HERE.

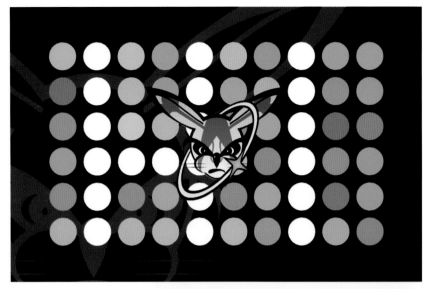

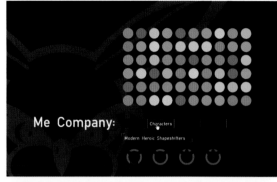

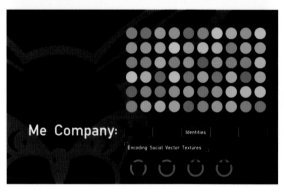

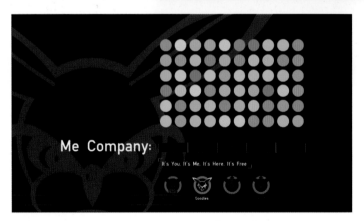

title
me company
URL
www.mecompany.com/
Design firm
me company

Bright colors that all work as buttons trigger sounds that can be used to make your own "song." (Although it may not be the best-sounding song you've ever heard!) This site uses Flash's sound-loading capabilities to their fullest. Every page has distinct noises, some fun, some annoying.

Title
yster

URL
yster.just.nu

Design Firm
SLB interactive

Yster features a great interface that loads quickly with nice, crisp movements. The three simple buttons have sounds associated with them. Overall, a good example of how Flash can create a simple site that maintains interest beyond anything frames could do.

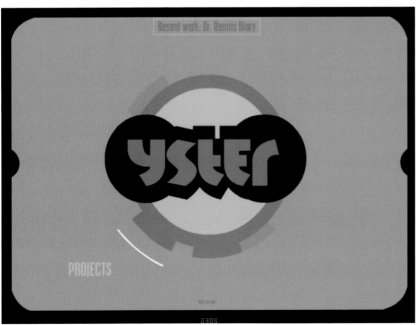

TITLE
  Kim Seng
URL
  www.freshdsign.com/kimseng
DESIGN FIRM
  consortio inc.
DESIGNER
  Kim Seng

Kim Seng uses a lot of effects that are used at other sites, such as icons following the cursor, but in fresh new ways. The movement is non stop, and it does take a moment to figure out which of the icons were buttons. Despite that, the site works. The black-on-white color scheme is quite appealing.

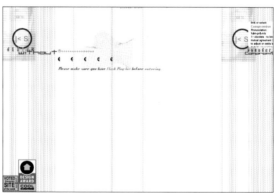

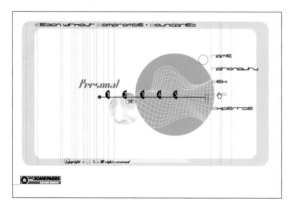

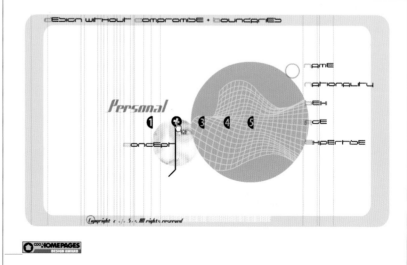

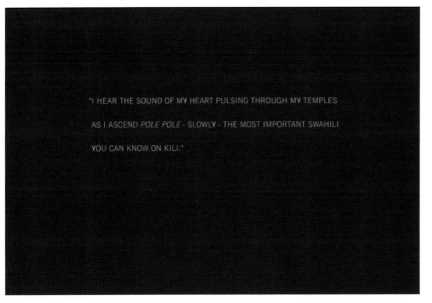

"I HEAR THE SOUND OF MY HEART PULSING THROUGH MY TEMPLES

AS I ASCEND *POLE POLE* - SLOWLY - THE MOST IMPORTANT SWAHILI

YOU CAN KNOW ON KILI."

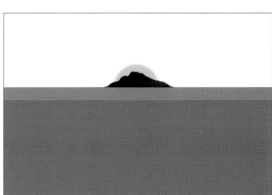

CROWN OF AFRICA

UNLOCKING THE SECRETS OF MT. KILIMANJARO

For generations, people in East Africa have turned to this, the 19,341-foot mountain that rises above the rest of the continent, and prayed. "Please God," they asked, thinking He lived on top of Kilimanjaro. Now outsiders flock to this trekking Mecca, to this piece of heaven on earth. Some are looking for adventure; some are searching for answers. Many will talk to God during the climb. Some will pray as they gasp for breath in the cold, thinning air of the mountain's summit. Kilimanjaro, the Everyman's Everest, is a seemingly easy climb. But about 10 people die each year. Join me as I prepare physically, mentally, emotionally and spiritually for this adventure. Read about the outcome of my journey in ESCAPE (Sept./Oct. 1999).

THE MOUNTAIN
CLIMATES, ROUTES, HISTORY, GEOLOGY

READY?
GEARING UP, CONDITIONING, HEALTH

GET OUT THERE
GROUP TOURS, GUIDES AND RESOURCES

INTRO | CREDITS
END EXPERIENCE

Title
crown of Africa
URL
www.crownofafrica.com/
Design Firm
Altrec
Designers
Gabe Kean, Dan Riley, Kevyn Smith
Programmers
Dan Riley, Enoch Platas

The climber speaks the text as it appears on the screen, giving this site's introduction an almost documentary feel. It would be impossible for sound like this to load in any way other than with Flash. Images of Kilimanjaro zoom by, adding even more of a movie feel.

Directory

3D Reality.net
346 Park St.
Suite C
Birmingham, MI 48009
info@3dreality.net
www.3dreality.net/main.htm

4 Guys Interactive
8203 Willow Place South
#230
Houston, TX 77070
dave@4guys.com
www.4guys.com/

52 mm
12 John St. #10
New York, NY 10038
info@52mm.com
www.52mm.com/

ABI Mouldings
3815 32nd St. NE
Calgary, AB T1Y 7C1
CANADA
markd@abimouldings.com
www.abimouldings.com/

Andy Lim
(Embedded Wireless Labs)
andy@artdirectors.com

Asmussen Interactive
Stubbekebingv 98B, 108
4800 Nykebing F.
DENMARK
ja@nethow.dk
www.turtleshell.com/asm

Chase Ace
(Petergrafik/Space Time Foam)
Brigadevej 28A 2th
DK2300 KBH S.
DENMARK
peter@petergrafic.dk
www.chaseace.com/

Crown of Africa
(Altrec)
50 116th Ave. NE
Suite 210
Bellevue, WA 98004
www.altrec.com
/experience/crownofafrica/
www.crownofafrica.com/

De+con/trol
(One Ten Design Inc.)
820 N La Brea Ave.
Los Angeles, CA 90038
contact@onetendesign.com
www.decontrol.com/deconv1/

DDBunch
(Diciamo Digital Buch SRL)
Pella Della Republica 1-
Bibliomediateca
05100, Termi
ITALY
ddbunch@ddbunch.com
www.ddbunch.com/

Dennis Interactive
(Dennis Publishing, Inc.)
1040 Avenue of the Americas
New York, NY 10018
info@dennisinteractive.com
www.dennisinter.com/di/
disite.html

Designgraphik
1011 Columbine Dr.
Apt. 1B
Frederick, MD 21701
mike@designgraphik.com
www.designgraphik.com/

E3 Directiv
311-1040 15 Ave. SW
Calgary, AB T2R-0S5
CANADA
kontakt@e3directiv.com
www.e3directiv.com/

Envision Interactive
987 University Ave.
Suite #22B
Los Gatos, CA 95032
insight@interactive.com
www.envisioninteractive.com/

Euro.runner SrL
Via Massarenti 190
40138 Bologna
ITALY
info@eurorunner.com
www.eurorunner.com/

Eye 4 U Active Media
Schwere-Reiter-StraBe 35
Haus 7
D-80797 Munich
GERMANY
info@eye4u.com
eye4u.com/home/index.htm

First 9 Months
(12 South.com)
209 10th Ave. S
Suite 340
Nashville, TN 37203
joe@12south.com
www.first9months.com/

Gobler Toys
1 Oak Ave.
Tuckahoe, NY 10707
iragobler@goblertoys.com
www.goblertoys.com/

Heavy.com
141 West 41st St.,
3rd Floor
New York, NY 10036
www.heavy.com/

Hensel Hauser
1867 E. Hamlin St.
Seattle, WA 98112
todd@henselhauser.com
www.henselhuaauser.com/

Human Evolution
Department of Anthropology
University of California,
Santa Barbara
Santa Barbara, CA 93106
walker@sscf.ucsb.edu
www.sscf.ucsb.edu/~hagen/
crania/

Hyper-Active
(BSI Media)
P.O. Box 262
Ojai, CA 93023
russ@bsimedia.com
www.bsimedia.com/

Iconiklastique Design
Klinik, LLC
1932 South Halstead St.
Studio 502
Chicago, IL 60608
e-mail@ida-a-ok.com
www.ida-a-ok.com/

Insomnious, Ltd
P.O. Box 300
London, HA1 3SP
UNITED KINGDOM
nosleep@insomnious.com
www.insomnious.com/

IShopHere.com
722 Randle Ave.
Nashville, TN 37202
ccormichael@ishophere.com
www.ishophere.com/

Jon Duarte
Communications
3230 Overland Ave.
Suite 124
Los Angeles, CA 90034
design@jonduarte.com
www.jonduarte.com/

Juxt Interactive
858 Production Place
Newport Beach, CA 92663
info@juxtinteractive.com
www.juxtinteractive.com/

KMGI.com Inc
350 5th Ave. 4913
New York, NY 10118
inquiry@kmgi.com
www.kmgi.com/

Lambie-Nairn
Greencoat House
Francis St.
London SW1P 1DH
UNITED KINGDOM
www.lambie-
nairn.com/flash_go.html

Me Company
14 April Studios
Charlton Kings Road
London NW5 ZSA
UNITED KINGDOM
info@mecompany.com
www.mecompany.com/

Mediamax
Doukissis Plakentias 12
15127 Melissia
Athens
GREECE
info@mediamax.gr
www.mediamax.gr

Melon Dezign
2 Rue du Colonel Roll
75017
Paris
FRANCE
info@melondezign.com
www.melondezign.com/

MKSite
(Massimo Kunstler)
128 Via Salaria
00198 Rome
ITALY
mk@mksite.com
mksite.com/

Mobley Media
7702 E. Doubletree Ranch
Rd. #300
Scottsdale, AZ 85258
mmobley@mobleymedia.com
www.mobleymedia.com/

The Multimedia Group
499 St. Kilda Rd.
Melbourne VIC 3004
AUSTRALIA
info@themmgroup.com
www.themmgroup.com/

Neostream Interactive
Gate 4 Bldg. 1
Riverside Corporate Park
105 Delhi Road
North Ryde NSW 2113
AUSTRALIA
info@neostream.com
www.neostream.com/

Netgraphic
(Audiobox Ulanghanzepte)
Iterdhurmstr 68
CH-8005 Zurich
SWITZERLAND
stagars@audiobox.com
www.netgraphic.ch/

Ntouch
(Random Media)
Prospect Row
87 Lansdowne Drive
London E8 3EP
UNITED KINGDOM
victor@randommedia.co.uk
ntouch.linst.ac.uk/

O2 Studios
987 University Ave. #22B
Los Gatos, CA 950232
spencer@o2studios.com
www.o2studios.com/

Obliviance
11 Ewart Road
London SE23 1AY
UNITED KINGDOM
rmiller@obliviance.ndirect.
co.uk
www.obliviance.ndirect.co.uk/

Online Interview with
Randall Larson
687 79th St.
Lino Lakes, MN 55014
gonzoz@mn.mediaone.net
people.mn.mediaone.net/go
nzoz

Party Flights
(Amphion Multi Media)
Vlaase KAAI 43
2000 Antwerp
Belgium
www.party-flights.com/

Petergrafik
(Petergrafik/Space Time Foam)
Brigadevej 28A 2th
DK2300 KBH S.
DENMARK
peter@petergrafic.dk
www.petergrafik.dk/

Pod New Media Ltd
49 Mount Pleasant
London WC1X 0AE
UNITED KINGDOM
info@p-o-d.co.uk
www.p-o-d.co.uk/

Raging Pixels
1000 Conestoga Rd., c-266
Rosemont, PA 19010
www.ragingpixels.com/flash
/ragingpixels.htm

Resonant SrL
Piazza G Mazzini 27
00195 Rome
ITALY
mail@resonant.it
www.resonant.it/

**Ricochet Creative
Thinking**
310-126 York St.
Ottawa, ON K1N 5T5
CANADA
www.ricochetcreativethink-
ing.co/

**Rullkötter AGD Werbung
+ Design**
Kleines Heenfeld 19
D-32278 Kirchlengern
GERMANY
info@rullkoetter.de
www.rullkoetter.de/

Timeticker
(Zwernemann)
Gaisbuehlstrasse 2
79725 Laufenberg
GERMANY
martin@zwernemann.de
www.timeticker.com/

Typographic
443 South Cochran Ave.
#201
Los Angeles, CA 90036
jimmy@typographic.com
www.typographic.com/

Varazdin
Kurelceva 22
42000 Varazdin
CROATIA
veljko.sekelj@vz.tel.hr
www.2000.varazdin.com/

Wojtek
(Perplex GMBH)
Sauerbruchtstr 1
97375 Munich
GERMANY
wojtek@wojtek.com
www.wojtek.de/

**Wolvesburrow
Productions**
2045 Wildwood Lane
Hanover Park, IL 60103
heydt@wolvesburrow.com
www.wolvesburrow.com/

Yenz
via Mercadante 8
20124 Milan
ITALY
yenz@yenz.com
www.yenz.com/

Yster
(SLB Interactive)
Stranden 3a
Aker Brygge
NORWAY
oystein@slb.no
yster.just.nu

About the Author

Richard Karl Danielson is a freelance writer and artist living in Cambridge, Massachusetts. He has produced live theater, cut a record of his own songs, and written for a variety of media–electronic and print. He studied history and writing at Marlboro College. He is a Web designer by avocation and is fascinated with the current Internet revolution. He is currently producing a short movie for the Web and writing a book on cinematography.